Eau Claire County Jail: A "Days Of Deliverance" Diary

Pierre Parker-Spencer

Published by Pierre D Bowdry, 2024.

This is a work of fiction. Similarities to real people, places, or events are entirely coincidental.

EAU CLAIRE COUNTY JAIL: A "DAYS OF DELIVERANCE" DIARY

First edition. March 4, 2024.

Copyright © 2024 Pierre Parker-Spencer.

ISBN: 979-8224001828

Written by Pierre Parker-Spencer.

If you think you're weird, read this! I think I have you beat! If you can understand to concept or think you get the puropse, let talk about it. You matter!

May 13

May 13, 2023, it's my second Friday, I meant Saturday here in this jail, Eau Claire County. So, I'm about 17 days sober from Fetti. The next court date is on the 15th of the next month which will be June, tomorrow being the 14th of May, Mother's Day. "I'm a terrible son'" the thought in my head. Every time I'm locked away from my mother and brother, even my street family/ relatives that I met while on the streets. This life is getting exhausting, 28 years of age, and I don't want to turn 29 inside a cell. I got a feeling about this year. Perhaps, I will finally kick this habit and/or way of life that I live. This being me walking away from the addiction and life.

17 days, A Recovered AD(Addict)

May 14

May 14, 2023, 18 days since I've last gotten high off the fentanyl. I'm watching American Idol right now as I write this. This singer's name, Megan, is a beautiful voice. I want to try out for American Idol. A "Recovering Addict" could leave a mark in this country. Today I made it again, another day, this is the only gift I can give my mom. Sobriety, cleanliness from drugs. Even though I can't touch you, I am still hugging you for Mother's Day through Spirit. I send my spirit and the spirit of the Most High to comfort you today. I'm blessed I have a younger brother of God to be there with you on this day. I love you. I love yall. I miss yall every day.

May 18

It's been a couple of days since I've last written I've waited for the right time, or should I say, "I'm at peace at least, while I'm on punishment." No, I am not happy where I'm at physically, however, I'm spiritually, and mentally about where I've came from. Today is my 22nd day of sobriety. I am at the number 22 itself. I remember being that age, if I was able to warn that man (young man), the turns he took going up and down in the years after, the years coming his way. Had that happened, no way would I be here writing this right now. I would warn that 22-year-old before to be aware of the "frenemies," the fake friends, parasites of UP and DOWN. I would slap that needle out of his hand. I would have slapped the straw away and the foil. When I think about the journey he went through, I realize the journey has built strength, character, and knowledge. Wisdom gained from the years. I would also apologize to him, letting it be known that he still ends up on the right path. I would tell him, "Do it again," "Don't change a thing." It's because of him. I'm here writing. Another day of deliverance, another day clean, sober. Another day at being at peace, trusting God in my situation, for he has not failed me. Nor has he ever, even when I was being a shit out here, a bad child, or One should say disobedient, not wanting to submit to authority. Trust has ruled my life. I put this here before me and God, and anyone else who may read this. I don't want "trust" to rule me, and I will trust God, my destiny, and my loved ones, I will trust. I lay that here.

P.S - 22 feels Great, A Recovered AD May 18, 2023

<u>May 19</u>

May 19, 2023, I would like to thank my Lord, my father for another day of deliverance from sobriety, and cleanliness. I need to do something before God and myself. I wrote this down on my list that day. This is to my Uncle Mo. I remember that day, it haunted, troubled, and broke me. I've lost my favorite person, a mentor. I know I've screwed up; it wasn't out of spite. The whole situation was confusing and chaotic. I wanted to tell you my silence wasn't helpful, it was hurtful, just know I've never meant to hurt, disrespect, and make more chaos. It wasn't that I couldn't tell you anything. I was expecting someone I shouldn't have trusted in the first place to do the right thing. Which is I messed up, I get it now, what you were trying to say to me. "Be a man, advocate, speak for myself." "Run my own life, the life God has designed for me, be a leader!" I didn't get it. I get why you are disappointed in me. I would like to apologize to you for all my shortcomings. I would like to restore our bond, I miss you, Uncle Mo. I'm tired of not being able to have my mentor in my life. I don't know if you will ever see this letter to you, or should I say I don't know if you would read this if I gave it to you, or ever had given it to you. I still have hope, that our bond will overcome the strength of 1,000 men, with infinite promise. The letter to one of my favorite people, I miss you, I love you. Thanks for all that you've done for me, from your nephew Urkel.

May 19, 2023, A Recovered AD

It's day 25 of deliverance. It was over three years ago. I was almost 200 pounds, well about 180 at the time. I was sober and didn't need any subs (suboxone) at all. Didn't have anything for any withdrawals because I didn't need it. I was incarcerated when my 25th birthday came into existence. I was depressed on that day. I felt ashamed not being able to celebrate but also celebrating my 25th inside a cell. My younger brother, my first baby, it will be his 25th birthday by the end of this month, the 29th of May. I won't let missing it define me or make me feel ashamed. I'm happy that he doesn't know this life, I will have it like this every time. What I mean is that my brother is free and does not ever have to celebrate his birthday in this "hellhole." However, I'm still at peace because he knows where I'm at and knows that I'm clear. I know he misses me and prays for me every day. I'm blessed to be alive to write this. 25 days of deliverance, I feel amazing, healthy, and better than all of the other times, I've overcome that sadness, of fentanyl.

Day 26

The 26th day of deliverance, May 22nd, 2023. I wrote haiku earlier today describing me at the moment, in "Awe," One would say. I titled it "Another Time," I think it's perfect because it summarizes the moment I was having. I had something to write and at the same time, I didn't know what to write. I'm currently watching the Pando App, my weekly video from *Social Dallas Church*. I wanted to record this before I forgot or at least this is just a "thought." I'm going to start this video over or at least rewind it to what I know what was being talked about! Once, I'm done writing this on lined paper!

26! Part 1, P.S. - Be Right Back!

5

<u>Another Time</u>

May 22, 2023

Don't know what to write
I have lots to write really
But it's not the time

<u>Part 2</u>

This is still May 22, 2023. I've been praying and talking to God. My relationship with the Lord God. Feel the transformations, I see blessings coming, the "miracles" he's showing, not just me but my inmates here. I keep praying and I haven't stopped since I've come back to God. I've finished my video from *Social Dallas*. Christine Caine, an orphaned born, now an amazing woman of God, presented in this video, titled "Don't Look Back." I know that I've changed because he keeps answering us, I said, "us," because not just me. I'm currently in a bible study group right now while writing this. I would like to thank God for the blessings he continues to give me but us here in this place. Miracles continue to be brought upon before my eyes. I'm thankful, so thankful that he is my life, and also continues to reveal. My cellmates have blessed me well. "God is Good," my cellie said to me.

Part 2, Day of Deliverance
26! P.S. - THANK YOU GOD

<u>D.L.B, K.M.F! T.I.G!</u>

May 22, 2023

The Past is comfortability, being use to. "Don't Look Back or you'll be turned into salt." As I just wrote that phrase. My cellie, or should I say, my big bro. Said a couple of things. All I saw and felt was the presence of the Lord, my God speaking through him. It's what he didn't voice, I heard that too, the message hidden within. "Trust," "Trust in God," It's become, or another way saying is part of my motto, my motivational phrase. Past life is what I must stay away from, One must reframe. The background, behind, "Stains, wash them away." Remove, vacate my, our, sins, mistakes. Talking to the Most High, talking to him, HE ALWAYS HEARS OUR PRAYERS. One must admit NO MATTER WHAT, ALWAYS WITH ONESELF AND the Lord GOD, even if it's not before no one else. Life, Live, Learn, and Die, that the flesh. This vessel will GO! However, I don't want my SOUL to BURN. That's why I'VE FINALLY LEARNED SACRIFICES, I MADE THEM ALL MY LIFE, DESTINED FOR GREATNESS! MY WHOLE LIFE, BORN ROYAL, Many Times, my entire life, I ran away from the Throne, He's had for me. My debt is still OWED. I will continue to SERVE, My God, My FATHER, EVERY DAY I WAKE, Is an ANOTHER DAY SAVED, So I THANK Lord God before I hop down from where I'VE LAID, EVERY NEW DAY. STARTING, BEGINNING, I'M LEARNING, To BE BETTER, MY PAST ISN'T NO LONGER A HURDLE, STAINS NO Longer REMAIN. "Forgiven." I am through my Lord, my SAVIOR. So many times, leave and LEFTED. Patient and ALWAYS WELCOMING back HOME, No GRUDGES

HELD, SHORTCOMINGS, "IMMER NIEMALS, ALWAYS NEVER" FORGAVE, FORGIVENESS, DER THE MESSIAH, VERGEBUNG! WAHRHEIT TRUTH, Ich kann nicht Lugen, I cannot Lie! Gott, God! For Life! Für das Lebens! Erinnerst du, jedes mal! Remember every time! Just say, Nur sagen! Erst, first, "Dankeschön," "Thank you!" Ich KOMME NACH HAUSE!" "I'M COMING HOME!" "Zwischen Euch, Gott, und DU!" "BETWEEN YALL, GOD, and YOU!" "TRUST!" "VERTRAUEN!" "BELIEF" "GLAUBENS!" "DON'T FORGET PLEASE!" "BITTE VERGISST NIE!" "DLB, KMF! TIG!" On your journey. "DON'T LOOK BACK, KEEP MOVING FORWARD! TRUST IN GOD!" Remember ALONG THE WAY! IMMER! ALWAYS!

The Last Part of 26!

Hi, I'm back. I guess I didn't see this happening either. I didn't expect to write like this in one day three times, or in thirds! My desire and/or motivation, today has come from God. I asked him to continue to present miracles in front of me. Today I ask him to forgive me because it took me all day to realize this "transformation." Today all itself was a miracle. For I was blind, now I see! Hallelujah! Thank you, for another day, I'm blessed, we're blessed!

The 26th Day of Deliverance
MIRACLE MONDAY!
P.S. - Dankeschön, Thank You, AMEN! Part 3!

"The 27th Day of Deliverance"

<u>I'm Annoyed</u>

May 23, 2023

I'M ANNOYED, I'm a HUMAN, not some TOY.

Born a boy, Today a MAN

Everyday learning to live up to the NAME "MAN"

"PROPHET", no disrespect but I know I'm "SENT"

Non-TRADITIONAL, REBELLIOUS, If need "Total

CHALLENGING" "That WAY, I AM WHO I AM!"

Don't assume, don't quote me on this, because NEVER

SAID, "I'M PERFECT!" However, I have "Perfected

PERFECTION!" "ONLY THROUGH MY TALENTS

God, My

FATHER GIFTED ME WITH!" You're LUCKY if you

ever

Hear physically quote myself verbally like this.

I know, One knows "FAR FROM THAT!"

AMAZING ACTOR BECAUSE TV INSPIRED ME TO

MIMIC

WHAT I'VE SEEN ON THERE THE TITLE OF THIS,

I got

from Robert, wait! PASTOR ROBERT MADU Jr from

Social Dallas Church, Pando App, He preach this sermon

in the front of the Elevation Church, his other

church family, this TIME like WOW, WORDS

FLOWING

OUT OF ME THAT I CAN'T BELIEVE, "DRUGS STILL

COULDN'T DUMB ME DOWN." INCARCERATED, ABOUT

AN HOUR, THE PLACE I'VE HATED BUT LOVED WHO, NO

LOVE LOST, For ALL I'VE LEARNED to KNOW "I don't

REGRET the ROADS I've BEEN ON" NOR "DETOURED

FROM, SHAME, IN MY PAST OFTEN FELT, NOW

REANALYZED SUMMARY, DESCRIPTION" REASON

"BUILDING CHARACTER" TRAGEDIES Revisited, "SAME

EVENTS, DIFFERENT LENSE"

"INTUITION, SECOND SIGHT, THANKFUL FOR THIS GIFT"

ENHANCE my ABILITY to UNDERSTAND

"LOVE LIKE NO OTHER, NATURAL, TIMES WITHOUT FEELING FEELINGS"

3 more Ds to compete 1M of Deliverance

"I'M THANKFUL and THANK THE, EVERDAY THE LIGHT

FLICK SIGNALING MEALTIME NEW BEGINNING" Realize

my last quotations might cause "ASSUMED" and/or "OBVIOUS" comprehension

"THIS ISN'T BLACKANDWHITE!" and "THIS ISN'T RELIGION"

"2 Day, I'M 17 AGAIN, 5, 22, 2023"
Last ADDICTION PLEASE IN PARENTHESES
"WORDS, NUMBER, DATES, PROPHECY!"
My second poem TITLED, written in YESTERDAY the evening "D.L.B,
KMF! TIG!"
I "ENCOURAGE" YOU TO READ
TEN YEARS AGO, 18 YEARS OLD IN HERFORD, GERMANY "HEUTE,
TODAY" I STILL SPEAK "UNIVERSAL" WRITING THIS, the "METRONOME TICKING"
"MUSIC, to me IMMER, ALWAYS" is "MUSIK," "Deutsch" is "German"
"ENGLISH" is "ENGLISCH" I don't forget the "C"
"COURAGE, CONFIDENCE"
THREE Cs, FEAR and WORRYING ABOUT WHAT OTHERS THINK ABOUT ME
THEIR VIEWPOINTS HAS ME IN SOCIETY "COWARDLY"
"A CRIMINAL, THREAT TO AUTHORITY"
INCARCERATED CURRENTLY, WISCONSIN IN EAU CLAIRE COUNTY
"EVEN IN TOUGH SITUATIONS, I'M DELIVERED and HAVE "PEACE"
"WRITING ALSO A GIFT, the FATHER BIG G HAS GIVEN ME"
MY ANCESTORS HAVE TRUST BECAUSE OF "THEM" IN ME
"MY PAST DOESN'T TAINT MY PURITY"

I'M MY OWN BIGGEST CRITIC, So I can't hide my competitiveness, I've learned to "TRUST IN GOD!" TIG!

MIRACULOUSLY, PATIENCE STILL HAVE ME, ANXIOUS

LEARNING SOMETIMES, IT OK TO BE

"LOVE, LIEBE" Mein STRENGTH, DENGLISCH, "CAN ICH" REALIZED at 17, that LIFE was what I made

"MUSIK ALWAYS, I'VE HID WITH SECRETS"

BILINGUAL IS MY LIFE "DENGLISCH" "I AM A MUSICIAN, MUSIKER, BIN ICH"

CHAMPION BLOOD FLOWS INSIDE OF ME FUELSD BY PAINS CREATING MOTIVATION TO "LOVE INFINITELY"

"THIS IS MY DESTINY," it's in "GOD'S PLAN"

Watch and see, "I DREAM ABOUT A FUTURE UNITY."

Even when I was ADDICTED to FENTANYL in MN, TWIN CITIES,

MINNEAPOLIS – ST. PAUL

ABBREVIATED "MSP" has taught "Following"

Avoided positions to "LEAD," trying to avoid "FAILURE"

"CREATED FEARS TRAUMATICALLY"

"BEFORE MYSELF and BIG G," I quote "I'M ANNOYED"

Reason being "1 Y, 6 Ms, and 16 Ds until I'M officially 3 DCEs.

"Can't believe, IT TOOK ME THIS LONG," Quote ME!

"I'M SPIRITUAL, a M.O.G" a "MAN OF GOD"

"I'M ANNOYED I'VE RAN AWAY, I'M DONE, THIS IS MY CALLING!" CAN

ONE ANSWER THIS RIDDLE PLEASE
WHAT'S THE ABBREVIATION FOR "ENT"
I've learned to DO "FLAWLESSLY"

-The 27th Day of Deliverance!
P.S. - Creative Writing Certificate
In 1 D! Einfach! Easy!

"CW Certified"

<u>Day 28 of Deliverance</u>

May 24, 2023

I THANK GOD, My BIG G before I hopped down the bunk where I lay. I will get some REST today before school here in the morning. I haven't even finished my pretest yet. Before class ends, I WILL BE CREATIVE WRITING CERTIFIED. I got my haircut last night, so I guess I will be walking to class with a "Fresh Cut" as well. I will finish my Pretest and receive my CW Certificate. Just know my THANKS is to BIG G and his "Miracle in Me," the TRANSFORMATION, he's continuing to do in me. "GOD IS GOOD." It's the feeling of accomplishment.

Day 28 Part A

P.S. - Productive Mittwoch (Wednesday) Morning! CW (Creative Writing) Certified

<u>Day 28 of Deliverance</u>

Hi, again., Well, I've done it. I'm Grateful, Happy, and Excited. I've done what I have written. God's my witness, my EXPLANATION behind my GROWTH and CHANGE. "EVERY DAY I'M COMING BACK HOME." My way of saying, "RETURN TO ONESELF," "I'M RETURNING TO WHO I AM." "SPECIAL MOMENTS, LIKE THIS, WHERE I ONLY HAD TO GRAB PAPER AND PENCIL, LEAD is a LOVE I'M LEARNING TO AGAIN, REKINDLED." Because I know "DAMN WELL" if I wasn't CANNED, this would be in "INK PEN." The reason for my previous quotes, not meaning the last two. I must say it's been a while since I have "CHERISHED No. 2." It doesn't change whether it's SCRIPTION is or isn't REMOVABLE. I tell you something, this "BLACK OR BLUE, CAN'T NOR WILL NOT TAME THESE WORDS OF PRODIGY."

-Day 28 of Deliverance Part B

<u>Part C - Day 28 of Deliverance</u>

Today has been Amazing. I, next week, for school my next class I will be choosing my certification, I will work for, or EARN. I completed my POST- TEST also TODAY. It was God who made a way for me to go to CLASS twice. A total BLESSING, miracle unexplainable, yet is explainable, to "THOSE WHO CAN'T SEE HEARTS," or "BEYOND THEIR OWN EYES!" "STOP VIEWING PHYSICALLY!" Being a M.O.G (Man of God), These "EYES SEE MULTI!" EVERY DAY IS ANOTHER CHANCE, ALWAYS, SOMETHING TO LEARN" "SEEING THE UNSEEN!" ALL MY LIFE, THINGS I NEVER SPEAK. Quote this, "I plead the 5th, THESE STORIES, INFORMATION IS TO REMAIN DORMANT, LIE DORMANT, SECRETS STAY WITH ME!" "BETWEEN I AND GOD, MY BIG G!" "I'M THANK HIM SENDING ME TO ECCDF (Eau Claire County Detention Facility), this PUNISHMENT, SPARKED LIGHT, ENLIGHTMENT BEING and BRINGING HOME," "GROWTH," AND, "DELIVERY." YES, HE DID INDEED, THANKS BIG G." I can not lie, "I can't, no wait that WORD NO LONGER EXIST TO ME. I'm looking FORWARD to Next Week." I'm making myself a bit vulnerable but not weak. It's INSPIRING when she is reading these. This is SAVING ME! "I THANK YOU FOR ACCEPTING ME!"

-Part C – Day 28

D.O.D (Days of Deliverance) Diary

P.S. - EVERY DAY I COME HOME!

<u>29 Days of Deliverance</u>

May 25, 2023

Tomorrow, I will be about a Month delivered from Substance, chemicals, DRUGS, 30 days. I've talked to my BROTHER, my first, my BIG BABY. We've talked for fifteen minutes about that. I told him THANKS FOR PRAYING for me EVERY DAY. I know it was GOD with US as we talked, I no longer feel anything, holding me back or weighing me down anymore. "I FEEL CONTENT, PREPARED, READY TO WORK!" "RESTORED." I BELIEVE, AND KNOW THAT, DESPITE THE INCARCERATION, I'M BLESSED BECAUSE I'VE COME BACK HOME, I HAVE FINALLY BEEN ABLE TO ESCAPE! This "ESCAPE" to "SAVE MY LIFE, FAMILY." "I WILL BE AS PROMISED." I going to "SAVE THEM." "THEM NOT BEING SPECIFIC." I now, know this "CONTENT FEELING, INFINITIVENESS, BEING TOTAL DELIVERED." IMMER, ALWAYS comes and abled every day to progress with "IMPROVEMENT." Delivery grows constantly, God every day TRANSFORMS me, consistently IMPROVEMENT HEALTHILY. THIS IS TESTIMONY, Lord my GOD, "Haven't GAVE UP ON ME." Neither has "MY FAMILY." "THEY STILL HAVE HOPE, BELIEVE IN ME." "I'M BACK BABY!"

-29 Days of Deliverance

P.S. - "I WILL BE BACK, SOON!"

30 Days of Deliverance

May 26, 2023

I have written a song/poem today. I went to the classroom, so I could write it. It was another MIRACLE presented before me. I enjoyed it. Had time with the Chaplain, and we prayed before he left. I could tell he didn't know how to handle me. It felt weird, still the presence, energy with us BIG G. Sent him to talk, get to know, hear my story. This is part of my TESTIMONY. This Diary, Inspired Writing. Dream, TIME TO WORK TOWARDS TO ACHIEVE!

-30 Days of Deliverance

P.S. - "Testimony" Diary!

<u>Life Statement</u>

May 26, 2023

Life Statement, Life Changed, Transformation

Can Ich (I), spoken auf (in) Denglisch

I kann change die World, The Welt

Success ist not Glück, Erfolg is kein Luck

Weg gelauft Immer, Ran away Always

Ein Son I am, A Sohn Ich bin

Testimony and Prodigy

Back, Home, Gone, Zurück, Nach Hause, Gegangen

Truth, Wahrheit, Totally, Total

I am Fertig, Ich bin Done

Einfach, Easy, Transformation

Life Statement, My Life Statement

Needed an ESCAPE, Way-out

Never thought I would live this type of Life

Hitting Store, Fetti, Steamers

Plead the 5th, won't criminalize MYSELF

Spent my life hiding, PrinZ Bambi still shined in Darkness

Der Psycho protected the purity of his TWIN, so his Herz (Heart) never taint

Demons and Angels for PEACE can learn Cooperation

Gift to Understand, Good Souls don't always make it through, can be AGAINST EVIL still

Dream within Me, Close YOUR EYES try to feel, Vulnerability NO LONGER FEAR

FEAR KEEPS ONE from GIVING IN, Won't give up THEM, GOD brought DELIVERY, to me

Despite this INCARCERATION, Wisconsin, ECC, Eau Claire County

BACK, Return to ONESELF, Writing always been a GOD-GIFTED TALENT

In my HEAD, pB is SINGING, American Idol, been told should Audition

WHOLE LIFE DIFFERENT, WISDOM my God allowed me, MY EYES SEE MULTI

Love is STRENGTH, not WEAKNESS, Prodigal Son, I WILL BE

"Glaub mich, Believe me" Past Vergangenheit, Behind me, Hinter mich

Remember, Erinnern, Bitte, Please, God Gifted my Soul Eternally

I SEE UNITY

Life Statement, Life Changed, Transformation

Can Ich (I), spoken auf (in) Denglisch

I kann change die World, The Welt

Success ist not Glück, Erfolg is kein Luck

Weg gelauft Immer, Ran away Always

Ein Son I am, A Sohn Ich bin

Testimony and Prodigy

Back, Home, Gone, Zurück, Nach Hause, Gegangen

Truth, Wahrheit, Totally, Total

I am Fertig, Ich bin Done

Einfach, Easy, Transformation

Life Statement, My Life Statement

SECONDS SOON MIMIC DAYS, WEEKS ARE LIKE A SEASON CHANGE

F, E, T, T, I, THE STREETS, CONSTANTLY ANNOYING, SCREAMING SCHREIEN

DO YOU EVEN KNOW MY NAME, PROCRASTINATED IN THE FAST LANE

My GOALS, have not started yet, 3 DECADES about a YEAR and HALF

TIME, still a FAIR SHARE, My BIG BABY and FAMILY, WAITED TOO LONG FOR ME

ABANDONED now ABANDONING, What ONE do, is what they KNOW EASY TO COMFORTABLE

Not being is so AWKWARD, FLOWING is NATURAL, reason why LIFE is LEARNED

HABITS we all HAVE them, Depending, the type, there's a BALANCE, GOT YOU CONSTANTLY SINNING

IN THE BEGINNING ALWAYS FELT LIKE AN OUTCAST, KING COBRA, LOVE MAKE ME VICIOUS

BEYOND CREATION, Vergebung Forgiveness, SHE WITH ME, CHOSEN, FAMILY MAN

Somewhat a STEREOTYPE, yes ONE can

FATHER took AWAY the CHANCE

Father, Mother, Children, Light and Dark, why yall PARTISAN

HOW IT LOOK, Bait got me HOOKED, being BOOKED ENFORCED HEALING, FULLY CURED

ENSLAVED don't be FOOLED, CAN'T EVER ESCAPE SCHOOL, LESSONS learned

Events challenged ONE to ENDURE

PROMISED A FUTURE WORTH living TO, faith in the UNBELIEVABLE

HOPE to ATTAIN the feelings of the MIRACLE

Released looking at the journey went through CHANGE is what been the purpose of Life

Inspired by Passion, have DESIRES, DEPRIVED BEEN too LONG FROM WORK

VACATION IS OVER TIME TO WORK, THE FUTURE, HURT will be burned, HEART WILL BE

SAFE AT HOME, Tragedies Triumphed from, the WORLD will know, LOVE alternates, can be OVERTURNED

TESTIMONY INCARCERATION DELIVERED ME

Inside trapped, ONE however HAVE FREEDOM

Life Statement, Life Changed, Transformation

Can Ich (I), spoken auf (in) Denglisch

I kann change die World, The Welt

Success ist not Glück, Erfolg is kein Luck

Weg gelauft Immer, Ran away Always

Ein Son I am, A Sohn Ich bin

Testimony and Prodigy

Back, Home, Gone, Zurück, Nach Hause, Gegangen

Truth, Wahrheit, Totally, Total

I am Fertig, Ich bin Done

Einfach, Easy, Transformation

Life Statement, My Life Statement

F, E, T, T, I, SHOULDN'T MADE IT pass Twenty-five

Had been WITH the WHOLE TIME

BETRAYED, a RIDE-AND-DIE, On the RIGHT remained

GAVE UP from the REFRAINED, REGRETS convert to MISTAKES, learned to

REDEFINE things, BACKGROUND, non-factor, not an OWL, behind can't walk and see

INTEREST ABSENT to me, NO tickets to Behind the Scenes, don't listen when One speak, walking invisibly, DEAF and BLIND I'm TELLING THE TRUTH

MISGUIDED, Morray led in Quicksand

Expectations froze, walked across, not a toe sank, attempt Flawless

Flew over those Hurdles, Confidence become FIRE, fire made the WILL, achieving, feeling the PRESENCE Changes

ADRENALINE, so Infinite, BLESSED with the SPIRIT

JESUS CHRIST, the REASON, done with TREASON

PEACE, needed, now got One constantly cheesing

Heart was bleeding, EYES blind with visions

History tried to fix it, Too many details, perfection caused STUCK

Stationary same POSITION, next step made fear to be a LEADER

Lonely confusion, now (I) see distracted

Tomorrow never promised, Golden Child, they TRUSTED, couldn't shake INSTINCT

No worries already gave in, TRANSFORMED WRITTEN, EVERYTHING RELENSED

Experienced, PROTECTED, THE SON, YES guess I'm a BIG KID

Under him, Prinz, for him WILLING, "I'LL SAVE NATIONS"

BECAUSE "FORGAVE" "MUST DO THE SAME," Had to CHANGE LANES

FINALLY KNOW, THE PURPOSE in, WHY ONE HE CREATED

UNITY, CAN SAVE THEM, MEN, I MUST LEAD TOO

GOD PLANS enforced, his THRONE, can't hide STILL HE CAN SEE YOU

WON'T EVER WIN FOOLS, Life's SCHOOL, HE'S PRINCIPAL

Life Statement, Life Changed, Transformation

Can Ich (I), spoken auf (in) Denglisch

I kann change die World, The Welt

Success ist not Glück, Erfolg is kein Luck

Weg gelauft Immer, Ran away Always

Ein Son I am, A Sohn Ich bin

Testimony and Prodigy

Back, Home, Gone, Zurück, Nach Hause, Gegangen

Truth, Wahrheit, Totally, Total

I am Fertig, Ich bin Done

Einfach, Easy, Transformation

Life Statement, My Life Statement

Day of Deliverance 31

May 27, 2023

Memorial Day Weekend, today went smoothly, I'm laughing while I write this. These dudes are funny. I am serious when I tell you that you wouldn't understand unless they were here. You wouldn't believe we're in the classification, that is stated on the cards with our names because, wait, I just say something is happening here. I feel it, see it, and understand it. This ENERGY is calming the atmosphere. NEW and FAMILIAR, the PERFECT description, making this VISIT so DIFFERENT, USUALLY would've already tapped in, allowed MENTAL RELASPE, CONSTEPLATING DOPE HIGH PLANS. I DON'T KNOW WHAT TO TAKE PLACE, NEXT NOR NEITHER EVENTS, that will be SENT. I HAVE HOPE, I'LL MAKE THE NEXT PHASE. NOT AFRAID.

-31 Days
P.S - REGRAINED and SAVED

Day 32

May 28, 2023

Something happened to me this morning. Couldn't sleep and really don't know. While lying down flashbacks, got me to sit up and start writing. Haven't ever forgotten that day 6, 2, 2019, I can perfectly explain however won't be in the details, I'll summarize. I felt an energy, I thought it was "Skinny Stevens," I admit I was tripping. Still, the same difference, even when I revisited the event. I know now the thoughts weren't fiction nor high-driven. This story is the "Truth." However today I won't tell it. Promise you this for certain, I will share it no later than June 2nd the anniversary, amount years will be four. Need the time to write the tale. A man of my WORD, rarely failed, if possible, am flawed. Forgiven, confessed already before I and GOD.

Had to take a break, to go to the church service and continued writing after "Truth." Ending to say, made it through another day. By grace, I'll wake up, on Memorial Day, May 29, my brother, my BIG BABY birthday. I thank the Most High, my motivation is serious, learned from this guy, and allowed myself to heal from the inside. I can give that only because temporarily trapped, Gift with a call tomorrow, sober from all chemicals. Spiritual I'll be high, Jesus Christ through him, the Father Most High allowing experience without influence. To say Happy Birthday my brother. May 29, 2023. He will be twenty-five.

-Day 32
May 28, 2023
P.S - Good Night

Flashbacks

May 28, 2023

Flashbacks, I'm thinking, THE PAST IS CLEAR, UNDERSTAND NOW!

NO ONE WILL BELIEVE THIS, SOUND LIKE I NEED MEDS and TRIPPING

CAN EXPLAIN THIS FLAWLESS, WOULD ANYONE LISTEN

6, 2, 19 WON'T FORGET

I WAS SUPPOSE TO schrei, SCREAM

PROPOSING, bitte please "MARRY ME"

I HEARD YOU, I'LL GO TO HELL AND BACK FOR YOU, LIKE A SUPERHERO

For so long I FOLLOWED YOU, tried to MIMIC

YOU DID things, so I DID them

REMEMBER IN THE WATER WHEN I FIRST SEEN YOU

Heart INSTANTLY KNEW difference THE FIRST TIME

Long for your attention, DENIAL KEPT ME FROM ATTEMPTING THEN

Got a Chance, WHEN I CAME BACK FROM GERMANY to the Twin Cities

OUR BOND still REMAIN, A LOVE STORY

With "D," took you away from me, "d, r, u, g, s," also PROMISE me

Gave instead misery, I'm still here BECAUSE the Most High GOD

Remember your DEATH, June 2nd, 2019. On the BED, DEAD with myself

She spoke to me, I heard her voice, no one listened, arrested me, ended in HCMC

Psychotic thoughts in my head, hallucinating, heard talking, couldn't ignore

Paid attention, Police switched seats while driving me, never seen it

Was on display, the Light Rail at Franklin Station, ALL EYES ON ME, WHILE SHE'S EXPLAINING PAIN, I NEVER FORGET THIS DAY, had to erase, didn't realize "forget" wasn't written in the sentence before had to rewrite it to complete it all, went to classroom. Life Statement had to be ALONE, to get things done

LEARNED dissect this word "A Lone" one, CAN NOT DO ALL ON MY OWN

ABOUT A MONTH RECOVERED FROM WITHDRAWALS OF FANTANYL. I'LD RATHER LIVE FOR THEM, FOR GOD, and HER, HAVE CHILDREN. FEEL LIKE A FATHER AGAIN "YALL CAN HAVE ALL OF THIS," in ADDICTION I quoted that

"I'LL GIVE EVERYTHING TO BE A FAMILY MAN." FUCK EVERYTHING

WHEN IT COMPROMISE LOSING THEM, I'M STUBBORN, no cloning

LAST OF A DYING BREED, time to spread A LEGACY, SON OF PRODIGY, DONE RUNNING, A LEADER SHOULDN'T BE FOLLOWING, THRONE ACCEPTED

Flashbacks, I'm thinking, the past is clear, I UNDERSTAND KNOW!

NO ONE WILL BELIEVE THIS, SOUND LIKE I NEED MEDS and TRIPPING.

Can explain this flawless, would anyone LISTEN

2019 June 2nd won't forget THIS

I was SUPPOSE TO schrei SCREAM "AUNT T"

PROPSING "Aunt T," MARRY ME, BITTE PLEASE, MICH VERHEIRATEN

VERLEGT und BLIND, blind and CONFUSED

ICH habe dich GEHÖRT, I HEARD YOU

Ich gehe zur Hölle für dich, I'll go to hell for you

Come back, komm zurück, "KÄMPF FIGHT FOR LIEBE LOVE"

Redefine SUPERHERO, you're my Herz, mein Heart

CHILDren OF GOD, let's OBEY, answer our CRY

Promised Messiah "I WON'T LEAVE YOUR SIDE"

My Wife, MISSING Home, it's been YOU THE WHOLE TIME BABY

Feel like GOING CRAZY, DON'T KNOW WHAT TO DO. FROZEN from AMAZEMENT, THOUGHTS, ENERGY, and VISIONS, WRITING the HALLUCINATION

HEAR EVERYTHING AROUND, LIKE MY EAR at the MOUTH, ENVIRONMENT SENSED, FACING WEST, VISION SEEING EAST, SOUND like JOHN THE BAPTIST, EVENTS, EXPERIENCES, MIRACLES I'M LIVING, CAN FEEL THE FUTURE UNBELIEF, Not WORRIED ABOUT CHALLENGE, will SURVIVE because TRUTH HAVE NO HEIGHTS, AGAIN 2019 JUNE SECOND. FROM CRYING to AGGRESSIVE ANGRY reaction from NO ONE UNDERSTANDING, THE VOICE

INSIDE MY HEAD, EVERYTHING TAKING PLACE PREDICTING, NARRATING, what taking PLACE, like COULD SEE, CONSTANTLY WAIT to APPEAR, COMING TO ME

"THIS CAN NEVER HAPPEN TO ME," NO I DIDN'T BELIEVE, IF THESE AREN'T MINE, MUST BE PROPHETICIZED. ANSWER TO THE CRIES ARE SOLVE I'M LIEING, If I SAY "I FULLY BELIEVE," SOMETHING TELLING ME, SHE WATCHING ME, INFORMING, ALL EYES ON ME, It's feeling DIFFERENT as it WRITE

MY RIGHT SIDE of MY CHEST I CAN FEEL IT, NO PHYSICALLY BEING CLOSE ENOUGH can TOUCH ME, I'm TRYING TO LISTEN, SPIDER SENSES ARE TINGLING, "YOU TOOK THIS LONG TO NOTICE ME," SHE just said to me. Wandered, now back. Believe in TELEPATH, INDIGENOUS, "WHERE YOU AT?" the Question INSIDE, I know she HEARS or PREDICTED, ONE WILL ASK, "MINNESOTA" BACK THERE, 6, 2, 19, DIED AND ROSE AGAIN, THAT DAY THE ALTERNATIVE END, RE-LENSED FINALLY, KNOW WHY I AM SITTING HERE, FOUND the WAY to THE TRACKS AGAIN, PATH REDIRECTED, SPOTLIGHT won't DEER, IMMUNED BARRIER NO LONGER FREEZE PB, IN THE DARK CAN'T TELL, NOW IN THE LIGHT, STILL CAN BRING ONE, SEE THEM COMPLETE THEIR MISSION, TRUE PICTURES IN FRONT of LIVING, SHOWING now GIVEN, the UNBELIEF I FORGIVE IT

GOD knows I SINNED AGAINST HIM, TODAY ANOTHER DAY DELIVERED "LOVE ME PLEASE" "LIEBT MICH BITTE," IN FRONT OF THE WORLD I will SERENADE, SING "AUNT T"

FLASHBACKS, I'm thinking, the past is clearing, I UNDERSTAND yeah!

NO ONE WILL BELIEVE THIS, sound like I need MEDS and TRIPPING.

Can explain this FLAWLESS, would anyone LISTEN

2019 JUNE 2nd won't FORGET this

I was suppose to SCHREI SCREAM "AUNT T"

PROPSING "Aunt T," MARRY ME, BITTE PLEASE, MICH VERHEIRATEN

Verlegen und Blind, Confused AND Blinded

Ich habe DICH GEHÖRT, I HEARD YOU

Ich gehe zur HÖLLE für dich, I'll go to HELL for you

Komm Zurück, Come Back, Kämpf fight, LIEBE LOVE

Redefine Superhero, you're my HERZ, mein HEART

Children of GOD, let's OBEY, answer our cry

PROMISE MESSIAH "I WON'T LEAVE YOUR SIDE"

My WIFE, missing HOME, it's been you the WHOLE TIME baby

In front of the world, I'll SERENADE

The FIRE won't run out of FUEL

Spotlight a nonfactor, EVOLVED to IMMUNED

Please marry me, Bitte verheiraten mich

For you, I'll SING, SCHREI, SCREAM June 2ND, 2019

Flashbacks, the is clear, Understand, no will believe this

2019 JUNE 2ND, don't need meds, not tripping

No forgetting, listen, ich schrei I'm screaming Aunt T
Bitte please "LOVE ME"

<u>33 Days of Deliverance</u>

May 29, 2023

Hi, it's another day here. The Holiday weekend is now officially over. I'm content and approve of everything that took place. I've gone to the classroom twice to get space to write this poem/song. It's called "Love Me." My mind wouldn't stop at all, the words coming into my head until I wrote them down. My hand was controlled by the brain, or should I say mind. MY HEART AND SOUL couldn't LET GO. ALLOWED the words to speak to me. Telling a message inside, DECIPHERING the reason, it may sound like I'm going crazy, but THERE'S SOMEONE COMMUNICATING. FOR MY ATTENTION. "LOVE IS TESTIMONY," is the finisher for the second part. "It's perfect, I'm leaving the way wrote because the original has to stay. I know get carried away, however, I'm writing what THE VOICE is telling me to. Now I tell you what took place on MEMORIAL'S Day and my younger brother, my Big Baby's birthday. A MILESTONE, he turned 25 today, I'M THANKFUL, I've experienced this. Being able to hear his voice, not as his strung-out, "High Ass" older brother, nor as an Addicted older brother, but as his Older Brother that substance-free and only addiction is GOD, LIFE, FAMILY, and my MISSIONS. Those are the ONLY INFLUENCE I need to be EVERYTHING I can. I had nothing but GOOD things to share while on the phone. We talked for about ten minutes. Before the call ended we both had a chance to pray like back then when we were younger. Ok, I'm overestimating, I can admit, I'm just trying to say, "It's been a while," that's all I'm saying. All I know right now as I write this, sitting up in my bunk at night, my cellmate is sleeping. I need to finish this project that I started today, so I can sleep, and pray God gives me another day to wake up. Better every day of Deliverance. I feel I can do anything.

Love Me

May 29, 2023

Flawed against God, everyone sinned, Jesus Christ the Lord only through him

THANKFUL EVERYDAY, SINS FORGIVEN, washed away

BEGOTTEN SACRIFICED the MOST HIGH FATHER a relationship with THE THERE'S a WAY, The Lord, our SOULS be SAVED, not GUARANTEE to awake

NEW OPPORTUNITIES to CHANGE so WHY STAY the SAME

Total SANE, Vessels will one day FADE, ETERNAL the Spirit can stay

IMMORTALITY in a way, that GOOD to me, won't say "I MISS YOU," TOO Love me, the only thing should be said, you're my strength, confident serenade heals

Love me, love me, love me, love me

Tomorrow not promised, nothing guaranteed

EVERYONE GOES TO SLEEP

ONLY thing JUST SAY "LOVE ME"

UNTIL WHEN I'll SEE you AGAIN, TRAUMFRAU du bist, you're the DREAM WOMAN, CAN PATIENTLY WAIT, when YOU'RE STANDING BEFORE, will KNOW THE MOMENT, BEING my SENT, WERE MEANT TO

CROSS PATHS, A SON of GOD, PLANNED PRODIGY, his LEGACY, the WORLD WILL KNOW REAL PRESENCE, the WORD I'll SPREAD, KINGDOM FOR THE will LEAD, THRONE ACCEPTED, TAKE YOUR HAND, FROM THEN will BE my QUEEN

NATION we'll GAIN for God's GRACE, SUCCESSFULLY be ATTAINED

For PEACE, CREATE a TEAM, WORTHY UNTIY, TOGETHER HAPPY we'll BE as ONE

THEY'LL HEAR US, my HEART will CAST the SPELL of LOVE to ACHIEVE MY PURPOSE the REASON God CHOSEN ME to REUNITE

LIVE this FIGHT to SURVIVE, the TEMPTATION OF EVIL WARFARE

WON'T win nor STAND AGAINST the LOYALTY, our DEVINE BOUNNDED INFINITELY, THIS LEADER CAN SEE a FUTURE dream, with ROYALTY

CHAMPION BLOOD born with INSIDE, the TITLE will be HIS

WIN HOME with PROMISE of HAPPINESS, THROUGH the MOST HIGH GOD

For the DREAM, FULLY HEARTED his work, HE will CHANGE ALTERNATING the spell of love, HIS DESTINY to REACH his ride and die, to COMPLETE

Under THE, a PRINZ must be UNASHAMED to reach, MUST SING, PROPOSING to her

ROMANTICALLY to BREAK the CURSE, HISTORICALLY through JESUS CHRIST, SHE can APPEAR TO HIM

Crown the Prince, BIG G MENTORED him to lead, HEAVEN have sent BLESSING to say TRUSTING ONE to REACH the WORLD, will RECIEVE the VICTORY, BE labeled KING to be PROVING the CREATOR CAN do THINGS the PLEASE, just BELIEVE you can do ANYTHING achievable

IMPOSSIBILITIES, DON'T EXIST to him, JUST HAVE FAITH through GOD

THE SPIRIT can ERASE PAIN ENDURED a long THE WAY

REWARDS in the END, ANSWERING CRIES, the STORY unbelievable TRUE FAIRYTALE

"Love me," WE'LL sing, UNIVERSALLY songs of LOVE ANOTHER

HAPPILY EVER AFTER, is ULTIMATELY COMPLETE the NIGHTMARES

All things, EVERYTHING WILL CONFESS, One as a whole

For eternity so she hears telepathically, BECOMING WHOLE again

To her One will sing, WINNING her heart, this Golden Child

ALL HEARTS will watch, to my wife serenading SAVING our souls

EVERYTHING, ETERNALLY, proposing a PROMISING

Jesus Christ the Lord, perform miracles like God the Father

With her together, we're SOULMATES, won't ever abandon my riders

My Queen, mimic the MOST High, give her desiring GODLY LOVE

The Immortal bond between a man and a woman DESERVED

End RESULT, ALWAYS guaranteed to WORK, HURT AND PAIN WILL BE EXTINCT

Miracle I'll redefine, change a story, our love is testimony

Day 34 of Deliverance

May 30, 2023

Hopefully, I will finish this before it's time to lock inside our cell. Another day endure and made. Tomorrow is Wednesday, I'll have school, and I will have the physical proof and certification for Creative Writing. I plan on getting at least three total by the time my next court date appears. I'm praying for a miracle; however, I'm not denying the crimes created. I must face the hole I've dug. We had a pretty decent day even though Glen and Pooh beat us in spade again. It was fun though. We'll get them next time for sure. The elders did put us in our place. It's kind of funny, I'm laughing inside my head while writing this. It's now 21:32 or 9:32 pm. My next will be Parenting, which will be certificate number two.

-D.O.D 34 P.S - CT # 2

May 30, 2023

Superhero your Messiah I will be, All my life for you, wanted to serenade

"I miss you," Every day when can't see your BEAUTIFUL FACE

To hold you in my arms, for the better I will change

Gotten lost along the way, can't run away from destiny

Deciphered the code understanding the next action to this scene

Blessed Spirit, impossible I can overwrite

Trust in God, I do, he is real, the Truth

My Heart longs for you, my Peace Stone, infinitely my juice

Use telepath to reach with belief, with all eyes on me

In Spotlight PrinZ Bambi, won't freeze

You're the fire, the first girl that make me feel like a King

Mystic Lake, that day I feel the feelings from the memory, answer to my prayers, you're the peace

I will close my eyes, try and see, indigenous to the core

My Dream Girl got confused, first time look in your eyes, swimming

Didn't drown, focused, kept following, back then, in the pool you marked me

This time Wifey, I right in sixth grade, I knew

If front of Everyone, I want you

I covered up with, "Do you have a phone?" meant to ask, "If you were with anyone?"

I texted to be locked in, should've wrote, "Can I be your boyfriend?"

There years too late to send the message, yeah

"One day I'll sweep you off your feet!" A Man of my word, meant what I said
Propose to you anywhere, close my eye to find your energy
Heyy, I'm in jail in Wisconsin, county of Eau Claire
Forgive me the whole time, Apologize, letting fear run my life
Didn't want rejection from you, silence gotten you taken away
I am here, confident without fear
Tried to hide secrets from you, finally realize you knew the whole time
I always wanted to marry you my Best Friend, birth year, the same
Learn to sing riddles, with thoughts find the beating of your heart
Know because now the peace it brings when I've successfully found, always an IQ
Indigenous Queen, por favor, bitte, please
Bebé, baby, my Königin, mein Queen
"Möchtest du mich verheiraten?" "Would you like to marry me?"
Die Frau meiner Träume, The Woman of my Dreams
Por favor, bitte, please, mich lieben, love me, die Warheit the Truth
Ich liebe dich, I love you
Ich will liebe machen mit dir, I want to make love with you
Wake up jeden Tag, every day, next to you
Want to be your last, the Champion of your Heart

Day of Deliverance

6/2/23

6, 2, 19, I saw my alternative end. On my death bed, the whole time I've heard a narrator in my head a woman's voice, predicting everything, events to take place. It start with a presence and/or energy I felt and swear it was so familiar that it confused me, I knew they were near watching. I embarrassed myself. Instead of playing my role and singing like I was supposed to do, I ended up in the psych ward, special needs. I'm not mental, I'm a healthy individual because GOD's delivered me, I know the purpose of my life. It's been music, promised the Lord Jesus Christ I will, and to present a miracle that asked. Send my Königin. America Got Talent, I can win it, if that's what I must do, to win her Heart, no way, I won't lose, prove to the whole world. Transformation of the MOST HIGH GOD SON. I am SOZO.

To save, I will deliver yeah, those that need I'll heal, singing to preserve, I will do well, asking GOD for my Queen Königin bitte please to me, make me whole again. Just say, "I do," sag nur, "Ja klar"

Ok, I confess. I'm upset that it took this long to figure out, however I already knew somewhat. I'm in rehabilitation. I'm ready to change MY LIFESTYLE. I have been in this cell and moved the to Special Area here, where I can harness the Gift that GOD gave me. I'm hoping that the MOST High make a way for me to get another chance. I am still confused however maybe about what's going on. Ok, I need to remember T,I,G, Trust In God, and keep singing with my heart. That's what I'll do until my time. I need to finish The Alchemist because once I pick the Holy Bible I won't read anything else, except the things I need for school, here because I need to get a couple of certificates before I'm back out in the world. Until that happens, I just going to play my role too. Just know when it's time, I'll be ready because now I know that I must SHINE MY LIGHT, be a Man of God, the FIRE WON'T BURN OUT. I must obey my Father Full-Hearted because I'm not supposed to be here. I was supposed to die four years ago, on June 2nd,2019.

-P.S - My Death
Alternative End

<u>Day of Deliverance</u>

6/3/23

Hey, how are you doing today? Mine is smooth right now as I write this. I have a beat in my head. I'm content with my life by the time I leave this, I will have written enough for a small book/diary. Now this is where I must let you know that I am the next best thing in Music and Entertainment, I also have Twins. They are a duo of princes, one of light, one of darkness unified for a promising goal to reach Peace, trusting in one human being. That's me, I will change history, and that is why until I get the chance, I will only read the Holy Bible, once I am done reading "The Alchemist" because why read a book someone writing when they could be reading mine. Also, I am a Man of God, which means my commitment is to the MOST High Creator, and Jesus Christ is my savior. I must write this down right now my is to be "The Prodigal Son" and use gifted talent to serve and "SOZO," which means in Greek "to save, heal, deliver, preserve, make whole." To those that need it. Now I am in transformation, the next steps are waiting to be made. My past is behind me now, I can enjoy and prove that there is God. Mind, body, and soul are "ONE." To work it takes trust, so as long as I believe in God In Flesh, there's nothing that can't be done. That's why I have faith that Miracles and Fairytales aren't entirely fake. Fairytales have unexpected turns, like when Jesus Christ died and rose on the third day.

This is mine, I rose again on the second of June 2023. I sold my soul on the first and today I'm coming out of the darkness to let my promise be known. I am twenty-eight years old born in Chicago, Illinois, and lived in Milwaukee every summer with my grandfather until I moved to Minnesota with my mother and brother, where I grew up. I was almost married with kids. Our second daughter passed away; it was RSV that killed and the hospital HCMC (Hennepin County Medical Center) discharged my two-week-old infant while sick, she still had trouble breathing when they sent her home with us. I watched, holding her in my left arm while working on my music, her older sister in the highchair trying to imitate me with a microphone in her way singing along. I talked to both of them inside the womb. My firstborn is the reason I slowly started singing. Anyway, my second passed on December 18, 2017. I woke up to a phone call from my ex-manager but also a role model, someone I look up to letting me know. I know everything went black, I came back to being held by a family friend who I was with hanging and partying with the night before. I came out of the darkness because of them. I felt peace with her while crying. She also held my first baby. About two days later they released my children's mother beating thirty-six hours of probable cause hold over our daughter's death. Now don't jump the gun ok because I know her, I've slept with her. She doesn't move in her sleep even when she's been drinking. Now you know I can say this next, she woke up to our sixteen-day-old infant not breathing. She tried everything even asking the neighbors for help. I don't care what language anyone speaks, everyone understands "Help," "Baby," and "Police." Also, if that person is crying how can you walk away and not help them, especially a mother in need? Sixteen days with us is the total she's gotten to experience; she was born small on 12/2/17. I've been told there's a spirit with me and I know it her, she's even with me right now in Eau Claire Jail. She passed at our apartment, it "fucked" with our heads, really "fucked" us up.

Now I tell you this before I move on, this happened at my mother's place. Where my children's mother and I slept in the other room, we cried over our recently deceased second-born baby girl, God showed us his presence with a sign that she was with him. There were rings of yellow light, and large haloes that surrounded us too, I started talking to my children's mom. I had no control over my words. Our baby went to Heaven.

Life changed a lot since then, we both went back to addiction. The two worst ones for her it was booze, and I started doing methamphetamine, and fell in love with opioids. It became my "NEED." I feeling ashamed, allow myself to run away. I went to the streets, believe when I say, "Everything happens for a reason." I've also met some relatives who kept me safe in a way. I had lived winters in a tent. Stolen from stores, drove steamers, been in and out of jail, treatment, and temporary sobriety. I committed so many crimes I haven't been caught for. I was tired of being that way and needed an escape.

So, I'm here writing this right now, clear-headed, chemical-free, high from the Holy Ghost. I did not go back into my past too much. I was in darkness and played with suicide. Incarcerated currently in Eau Claire County of Wisconsin, despite that, I've received a blessing. All I know is that people talk about "rehabilitation" where I am at, it makes you go back on your life and think about your lifestyle. I went through withdrawals from one of the worst drugs. They didn't give me anything for it. I had to go through hell to get sober again. I also made a promise to myself and God because it's a different ball game here when in custody, you sit. That's why, I gave my life again and word that if I get another chance "I will change my life around." Also found my purpose, and God's Plans for my life that I will do and live out because "My Prinzessin," my firstborn is part of my future. She is the reason I will improve for the better. I will become a "Family Man" again. This is the Golden Child, the Prodigal Son, and the Master Performer.

D.O.D Diary

<u>Day of Deliverance</u>

6/4/23

Dear My Big Baby,

This is your older brother. I need to do something very important for me. This is what you wanted from me; you've always wanted to know if I had any plans. Here are some of them. I will provide you with information for my Facebook because I need you to log in for me. I need your help to reach someone special to me.

So, do you remember the female that I used to talk on the phone with while growing up? The Native female at Mystic Lake Casino, at the swimming pool. It was about a long time ago; I think you were in 3rd grade because I was in 6th grade then. Well anyway, her name is on the envelope. We're Facebook friends. I need you to message her from my account. It must say exactly this, "Hey, this is his brother. He is in jail in Wisconsin. His next court date is June 15th. He doesn't know if he's getting released or not, but he asked me to do this. He also told me to write you so, I can give you a letter he has written for you. He really wants to make sure you get this, that's why he sent it in an envelope with your name on it sealed. He knows I will make sure it gets to you without it getting lost. I was wondering if I can send it to your address and/or deliver it to you?"

Now once you send the letter please keep logged until she responds. If it's easier to send than deliver it then, ok but I really need you to do this for me. I don't know her exact address to it that's why I'm trusting you. The reason why I'm having you or asking you to do this for me is because it will impact my future. I'll just say her not getting this letter will change some things. I will tell you this I should wrote her it a long time ago. God has put her in my heart to write her a letter. Just know this, I put heart and soul into that. I'm back, so you know when I am serious. PLEASE DON'T LOSE THIS! ANY OF THIS AT ALL BECAUSE I'M TRYING AND DOING/TAKING ACTION TOWARDS CHANGING LIFE! I am not yelling at you, you're the ONLY I TRUST to do this. Once again if you can bring to her that, it will be way better but if it's easier to write the address on it and send it through mail for me, that will also be great. It should require no stamp just drop it in the mailbox, if it's getting mailed.

Anyway, bro, I miss you. I'm feeling amazing. I know where I'm at right now and current situation, but this opened my eyes. It made me give my life back to God, face my past, forgive everyone who hurt or did me wrong, ask forgiveness for my crimes and sins, and decide to change my life. I'm willing to go to a program to start fresh. I also want you to know that I'm working on my gifts/talents as well and I'm pursuing my dreams with Music and Entertainment. I've been singing, worshipping the Lord every day improving, the Holy Ghost is transforming me from the inside out. It's the goal eventually to audition for one of them shows and the world beatbox challenge, I'm that good. If I could call you I would but I am broke. I don't need no money because I have faith. Well, I'm at the end, I love you, bro. Pray for me. Bye!

Day of Deliverance

6/5/23

Hi, I had to take another day off. OK, I'm kidding, if you think I didn't write and believe me. I don't know how I should take it because there's something I write every day now. You have to remember I'm also a poet and lyricist. I'm a WRITER all together. So, did you realize that I've only written "Day of Deliverance" at the top? I'll explain why, it is because I want to prove that growth is every day, so every day is a chance, every day is a "Day of Deliverance" because everyone sleeps but, not awake. When granted, it should be cherished.

D.O.D Diary
P.S. - EVERY DAY

Day of Deliverance

6/6/23

Good Morning, I want to thank God the Father for allowing me to wake up. I've already done that and prayed over the first meal and read "Daily Bread" for today. The message was about how we all idolize things in this world, which says in the Bible, "You shall have no other gods before me." "You shall not bow down or worship them." He being our Lord, Creator, and Father, He forgives us. Do "treasure" things, desires, and even people. It also says, "showing love to a thousand generations of those who love [HIM]." [HIM] representing God. This is what I've learned this morning, it's okay to treasure as long as our hearts which he knows, truly loves [HIM] more than anything FIRST, we are always FORGIVEN.

<u>Day of Deliverance – Part 2</u>

6/6/23

Hi, successfully made it another day. Today turned out to be productive. So, to let you know I'm in the "Mental Health" Area or "Special Needs." The only special need I need is a double or extra tray and I'm not getting that met. So, I don't know why I need to be here because I'm a healthy person, for the most part, and that's a continuous improvement. Especially since I've been clean and sober from all chemicals and prescriptions. I didn't mention earlier but today was my Grandmother's Birthday, she passed away last year. I've not gotten to talk to her in the past few years but rather than mourn I am choosing to enjoy this day for her. If I wasn't a different person and wasn't a Man of God. I know I would not be writing this today. I miss her food, comfort, love, and her hugs, and kisses. My Grandma was ONE OF the FEW people I had a soft spot for no matter what. One thing for allowing me to be my own person or persons. Also, confidence and the courage to carry on. I could tell her anything that I couldn't no one else. No matter what, I was always her "PP." No one could change that. I am just thankful for the time I did have with my Grandmother and she did live a full life. She was almost 80 years old and got to see her GREAT Grandchildren, not many get that chance, nor make it that far in life. I know she's still watching me. Had a blessed day, I prayed before I wrote this. I have faith I will write again, until then.

D.O.D Diary
P.S - R.I.P Grandma Pat
Love You and Miss You!

<u>Day of Deliverance</u>

6/7/23

Hi, I've thought I should put this on paper before I go back to sleep until class starts. Now I don't know if I will be able to go but I'm leaving it in God's Hands. I thought it would be good to just manifest it or wire it in my brain that there's a way. Even if I don't make it, I know that I'll get there eventually to finish my certificate for Parenting at least I have faith in that. I've done my part in this, it may be misunderstood and sometimes that happens. I have come to the reason. I have responded with positivity, reacted the way I'm supposed to, and I understand other viewpoints of interpretation. All this is behind me, I now wait to move forward. I will see my teacher again in class before I leave this place, this jail. After this visit, rehabilitation this time have gave me a "scare" and opened my eyes. I won't ever step foot in this Jail ever again. I promise this with all my heart. "Fuck getting HIGH and doing ANYTHING THAT LEADS TO THIS HELLHOLE. Ich bin fertig! I am done!" I mean that "SHIT!" Lord God, please forgive me for my vulgar language. I NEEDED to put THIS on PAPER, Til Later.

D.O.D Diary
P.S - Wednesday AWAKE,
Eye Opener, Realization!

<u>Day of Deliverance – Part 2</u>

I just got done helping my friend here to send messages to be possibly moved to another area in the jail. I will be hopefully able to go to school today. I will be moved hopefully before 2 o'clock. There's always a way. I pray over the food I'm about to eat and I thank God the Father for continually blessing me. Praying, Amen. It's lunchtime, I will be back after I eat my food.

D.O.D Diary

Day of Deliverance – Part 3

I just took a shower to clean myself up and be ready to look presentable in Orange. I still have hope I can make it to class or school today. I already have my things packed so when they call my name, I can just put my things in the bag and go. I'm praying that things overturn. I know must stay patient and wait and just trust in God. This is what I do now, even if it doesn't work out, at least I will have an understanding.

D.O.D Diary
P.S - Patience

Day of Deliverance – Part 4

"The Alchemist," has turned out to be an amazing book. I know that God has sent the book for me to read. It is every time I can sit and focus and concentrate. There is always the perfect moment when it's needed. The last time was just before this diary entry I'm currently writing. What I've just read was about how God knows the future, it also talked about that God rarely shows us the future and that a future that can be altered.

I want to confess the reason why I took my second daughter's death so hard. I had a nightmare that woke me up out of my sleep crying. My children's mother, I didn't tell her what was wrong, but I knew it had something to do with our newborn about a week old at the time. I knew I saw her death in a way that scared the hell out of me. This is my first time writing ever and

50

I probably won't write this again. I didn't forgive myself when she passed because I felt I could have altered it. I felt something wrong when we had to pick her up and my children's mother at the hospital. I knew then that something was going to happen when I blacked out and saw red before coming back to while at the steering wheel with the car in park. I yelled, "She needs to go back up there!" Meaning we need to take her back inside the hospital. It didn't happen that way because no one listens to me when I say things without control, I was used to it. I held my newborn baby in my left arm and had her big sister in the highchair until she was able to sleep while I was working on music. Finishing my first album, "DengliSch A1bum." I finished the last song before she went to sleep. My firstborn, we had a connection through music. Every time I've worked on my music she would always crawl or walk and try to get my attention. I would always let her try to sing and play with the microphone with me. In her baby way, it would motivate me to keep pushing myself. Anyway, this was on the 16th which turned into the 17th. I was up that night because I kept thinking about bringing our newborn to the hospital. Something was fucking with my head. I kept hearing, "Take her back!" A voice kept saying that to me. Music was the only way I was able to ignore it. It was enjoyment when I finished, I looked at her, my newborn baby girl looking at me while holding her. I felt peace from her, and she was at peace watching me. That's why the tattoo I will get on my left forearm will have her timeline being 12/2/17 to 12/18/17 and her zodiac sign, which is the Sagittarius. I'm still going to do that to honor her, I know her soul is always with me. I now know the truth which is what I felt all along but I've learned to accept the things I cannot change and have the wisdom to notice the difference. I do miss her every day which IS WHY I NEED TO LIVE LIFE TO THE FULLEST, BE THE BEST I CAN BE because SHE LIVES THROUGH ME. Also, NOT EVERYONE AWAKES BUT THEY DO SLEEP! This is my June 7th confession. If I did things differently, things would be different now. I would be different too! T.I.G, Trust In God. T.I.M, Trust In Him. M.B.S, Mind Body Soul. T.T, The Trinity. Altered Future!

- Days of Deliverance Diary

"To All the people that has helped me while I was at my lowest."

Hey bro, I haven't seen the things you've done at your lowest, but I have in a way. This is also your lowest point, this Jail/Rehabilitation Center. This is both of ours. We both have grown in here, our eyes have opened, and our heads have become clear. I've NEVER TALKED TO ANYONE until I met you. I learned a lot from you and your stories. You are the proof that "Fairy tales" are real and can be true or come true. Everyone does the same thing in the system, when in the system but don't admit the reason why they're in turmoil, the reason is themselves. They put themselves here, however, I have seen you do the opposite. You realize and know you could've done things differently and that's why I call you Brother because you're human and a Good Man and I know you're a Great Father. I have faith that we will see each other do great things and improve, change our lives. Do positive responses to this to overturn our past to make it to AMAZING FUTURES GOD HAS PLANNED AND WAITING ON US. WE JUST HAVE TO GET THERE. You will be my only positive thing to look forward to when I get out this hellhole. You have an amazing family bro; I can tell and really do BELIEVE this. I also BELIEVE IN YOU! I'm the oldest boy in my mother's side and the only boy on my father's. I always wanted an older/big brother who could influence me and push me to do my best. Most importantly to motivate me, believe, and help guide me towards being successful, the best I can be. Encourage and teach and be a positive role model in life. I'm thankful that God made us cross paths, just know I'm not going to let you fall back either because I care about you and your family too. You're older than me, so you're MY BIG BROTHER, you're going to be the first I see when I get out. I love you too bro! Just know I will have the word search done by this weekend, but I know I will have to wait to give that to you when we see each other again. I BELIEVE AND HAVE FAITH about that future event becoming a reality. UNTIL WE SEE AND MEET AGAIN! Not ever in here! I love you K!

By Your Brother From Another Mother
P.S. - You're a Great Man!
Answer to my prayers!

<u>Day of Deliverance – Part 5</u>

Today has been a blessing. My brother from another mother got out of this hellhole today. It was after dinner but he's out. God turned the table today presenting miracles and answers of understanding. I accepted things that didn't happen. I can tell I'm changing because my thought pattern is thinking differently, learning to interpret even "no" as a reason for better plans. I mean, I may not have made it to class, but I got to see God overturn things for my brother from another mother. That was amazing to witness because it was unexpected even though I had a feeling about it, but I didn't when. This is why it brought me happiness because I have gotten to experience it with him the enjoyment of the GOOD NEWS! I have FAITH In the UNBELIEVABLE! I've thought I'll write this before I knock down another Chapter of "Re-Entry Success" before I pray and go to sleep.

D.O.D Diary
P.S. - See you again big brother! K!

Day of Deliverance

6/8/23

Today I will apply myself to the "Re-Entry Success" packet that was sent to me. It's the goal to finish it before this weekend is over which means I have until Sunday, the 11th of June. I know I can do it. Today's passage was about resilience and that is what I must have to complete this. I looking to grow in character which is always no matter how strong can always improve. This is how I plan to spend my morning, Thursday, June 8th, 2023. It's also my cousin's birthday.

Day of Deliverance- Part 2

I have applied all day besides the breaks for eating to the "Re-Entry Success" course. I'm about a quarter of the way there. I want and will complete this before the end of this weekend. I have good news I have written my testimony and my plan for the future. I know I will most likely go back to working on the "Re-Entry Success" packet I can at least finish Chapter 5 before I go to sleep. This will probably be my last entry for today. I have faith that God will bless me with another day. If not, then that's just my time. I'm thankful every day he allows me because I know he still has a purpose for my living. I also want to say Happy Birthday to my cousin "D.B." Hope you enjoy today! I love you and miss you, from Eau Claire Jail. Happy Wishes!

D.O.D Diary
P.S. - Praise the Lord!
Amen!

<u>Day of Deliverance</u>

6/9/23

It's Friday, early morning/twilight, just before sunrise. I'm guessing, I cannot see outside because I'm incarcerated. I just wrote an obituary and a mission statement for my life purpose and future end goal. I could not sleep much however I woke up with answers. I'm thankful for another day to improve and apply myself for transformation and change in my lifestyle. I'm looking forward to taking action and fighting for a future, the right way. This is my morning and starting entry for Friday, June 9th, 2023, another "Day of Delivery" given by God. I'm going to rest up because I'm applying myself to "Re-Entry" again this Friday morning.

D.O.D Diary
P.S - Friday Morning

"IT IS WRITTEN"

<u>God's Maktub</u>

<u>IT IS WRITTEN</u>, maktub
Fatima, a woman of <u>THE DESERT</u>
So, <u>I MUST COME</u> back
<u>TO</u> because you are my Fatima
<u>SO I CAN BE</u> your man <u>ENOUGH</u>
For my Fatima, a woman of the desert
<u>TO PROVIDE FREEDOM BECAUSE</u>
Fatima, a woman of the desert
So <u>I MUST RETURN HOME</u> to you
<u>MARRY MY TRUE LOVE</u>
It is written
<u>LOVE ME</u>, that's <u>GOD'S MAKTUB!</u>

Day of Deliverance – Part 2

Hey, good afternoon, well about that. Today I tried something new and different I had to think hard about what I need to live a purposeful life like to maintain freedom from incarceration. Freedom to reach goals, and freedom to learn how to improve the chance of success. I learned freedom is the key and depending on the amount of freedom, one must effectively use the resources available to them. Doing that can make a difference in outcomes. Outcomes of freedom, incarceration, or the FREE WORLD where YOU can SHAPE YOUR own FUTURE and BOUNCE BACK SO YOU CAN GET TO THE THINGS THAT MAKE ONESELF WHOLE. I wrote my Plan for my first six months after being released from correctional. The goals I want to reach towards My Dreams and future. I realized the change in my thought patterns and ways of understanding. They're improving the way I handle things, the ability to cope in situations with the ability to make smart decisions. I can only control myself and the things that God my father allows me to do. Learning and realizing this has taught me how to have TRUST, PEACE, LOVE, KINDNESS, PATIENCE, and how to be GOOD. Despite the odds and obstacles, I can OVERCOME and SHINE ANYWHERE EVEN in the DARKEST of PLACES. Lunch was great today. I'm going to pray, take a shower, read some of the "Alchemist," and WORK ON MUSIC. In that order until supper. After I use the can from having too much water.

D.O.D Diary

P.S - Productive Friday Morning

June 9th, 2023

"Maktub" IT IS WRITTEN

6/9/23

IT IS WRITTEN, Maktub!

Fatima, a woman of THE DESERT

So I MUST COME back

TO, because you are my Fatima

SO I CAN BE your Man ENOUGH

For my Fatima, a woman of the desert

TO PROVIDE BECAUSE Fatima, a woman of the desert

So I MUST RETURN HOME to you

MARRY MY TRUE LOVE

It is written

LOVE ME, that's GOD'S MAKTUB!

Do not matter what they say, ignorance

God the Father talks to me, writing is our system

Made a promise to change my lifestyle, I asked for a MIRACLE

Things start to become clear, VISIONS AND DREAMS

The TRANSLATION now EXPLAINED, so LIVING For HIS PURPOSE

Learn to realize when FOCUSED, I so AUTOMATIC, Bill Kaulitz

MOVE like Goku NATURALLY, in Ultra Instinct

FLOWING WITHOUT FLAW, feel LIKE my power level is Infinity

Red hair, Super Saiyan GOD mode, Michael Todd "Crazy Faith"

Jesus Christ, my Lord was a God HIMSELF, breaking barriers to unify

WHEN I THINK OF YOU, see a future with you by my side

It is written, Maktub!

Fatima, a woman of the desert

So I must come back

To, because you are MY Fatima

So I can be your man, enough

For you Fatima, a WOMAN OF THE desert

To provide freedom because Fatima, a woman of the DESERT

So I MUST RETURN home To YOU

Marry my first love

It is written

Love me, that's God's MAKTUB

Took me 16 years, it's all clear

Never should've let fear keep from messaging

You "CAN I BE YOUR MAN?" and "I LOVE YOU"

SINCE THE FIRST DAY, when our paths crossed

I laid eyes on you, Mystic Lake Casino swimming pool

Learned to swim after MET YOU magically

Just to get next to, overcame, no worrying

I'm marked by your spell, love potion

Had no control of my actions, impulsive

Self-control of my emotions, WINNING freedom

Peace and knew God sent you answering

Prayed, cried, and wept for A Woman blessed with BEAUTY

Felt I am lucky, to an Angel, to be allowed around

"One day, I'm going to sweep you off your feet!"
Grab your hand, change your life, make you a QUEEN!
PLEASE, it is written MAKTUB
Fatima, a woman of the desert
So I MUST come back to because you are my Fatima
So I can be your man, enough for you Fatima
A woman of the desert
So I must RETURN HOME TO you
MARRY MY FIRST love, it is written
LOVE ME, that's God's!
MAKTUB!

<u>Day of Deliverance</u>

6/10/23

I have experienced "Maktub." You would have to understand to know what I mean. God the Father gave me answers to my questions. Also, directions and guidance on what I need to do. To have/achieve earning a purposeful life gaining true freedom so I can provide freedom to others SERVING FIRST GOD and his Kingdom, SECOND my Queen being the Woman I love who will become MY WIFE, THIRD MY CHILDREN, FOURTH Loved-Ones like FRIENDS, RELATIVES, and my SUPPORT TEAM, LASTLY FIFTH, ANYONE WHO WANTS/NEEDS HELP and GUIDANCE TO BE THE BEST THEY CAN BE NO MATTER THEIR SKIN COLOR, PAST, CURRENT SITUATION, and HABITS. GOD CAN OVERTURN ALL THINGS. This is my Friday the 10th of June 2023 morning entry, message, and writing. Enjoy your day, also HAPPY BIRTHDAY Mom! I LOVE YOU! I miss you and HOPE TODAY is FULL WITH MIRACLES AND PURPOSE, I PRAY AMEN! I am FAITHFUL and WILLING TO WORK TO FINISH my GOAL, this weekend of "Re-Entry Success" FOR THE FUTURE MAINTENANCE, OF FREEDOM WITH EFFECTIVENESS! After a champion's breakfast and reading!

D.O.D Diary

P.S - Happy Birthday "B.A.B"

YEAR 1975, My Mother

Day of Deliverance 1

6/11/23

I have finished my 7 steps of "Re-Entry," but I'm not done yet. I must complete "The Action Plan," to complete and do what I can. I have planned to finish the "Re-Entry" at the end of the Weekend. I have faith in myself to meet the goal I have set. Monday, I will be able to say I'm certified in "Re-Entry." I just switched my spot where I was sitting so, I could watch The Flintstones while writing in my diary. I just thought of my cousin who used to say, "Silly Billy," he would say it when we were young.

I just took a break to sort out my clothes because I plan to take a shower after I finish writing this journal entry. I realized when I focus and lock on my target, I can be in a crowd of people and still do what I need to do. I am learning how to not allow myself to get distracted and concentrate on the objective. My ears can still hear what's going on so as long as I'm focused, God will make sure my other senses will work together as a team to keep me safe. This is transformation, education that evolves ONESELF to be a better form of self. I know I'm different and feel healthy, tenfold. God is Great! HE ALWAYS REVEALS, WHAT HE WANT TO BE KNOWN! THE LANGUAGE OF THE WORLD, IS THE SOUL OF THE WORLD. THE SOUL OF THE WORLD, IS THE SOUL OF GOD! BELIEVE, HAVE FAITH, TRUST IN HIM, AND YOU'LL BE ABLE TO DO ALL THINGS BECAUSE HE IS ALWAYS WITH YOU!

D.O.D Diary # 1

Day of Deliverance # 1A

It's about noon and lunchtime is here at Eau Claire County Jail. I realized the reason why today is happening. It's the day of and the moment to test if I want what I have written. If my heart and soul are really in it. "It's time to put my money where my mouth is." What I must finish is the last part of "Re-Entry." It's the "final exam." I have learned and know everything I need to know. It's within me and must focus, be prepared, and be ready to work to finish the final objective of this chapter, "Re-Entry." "REST," helps you recover from training, this way your mind will be able, competent, and ready for effectiveness to achieve your goal at the right time.

D.O.D Diary
P.S - ON TIME GOD
Sunday Noon

Day of Deliverance # 2

6/12/23

The sun is rising, I can see it from my little window that lets me know when it's night or day. I finished "Re-Entry," and signed my "ACTION PLAN," for success. All I know, is I don't want to come here again as a criminal, a prisoner dressed in Orange carrying a blue bag to go to a cell because I got to do "TIME," away from the Free World, my family, friends, and those who love and care about me. "Ich bin fertig! I am done!"

with anything that takes me from them negatively. I have learned the tools I need to succeed and I'm going TO ACQUIRE MY FREEDOM, SO I CAN LEAD AND GUIDE, GIVING LOVE, PEACE, UNITY, and PROSPERITY TOWARDS A PROMISING OF TRUE FREEDOM!

<u>LiebeLove</u>

6/12/23

Liebe, Love, Gut! Good!
Liebe, Love, Genug! Enough!
Liebe, Love, Ich bin! I am!
Liebe, Love, Gut Genug! Good Enough!
Liebe, Love, Ich bin, ja!
Liebe, Love, I am, yes!
Liebe, Love, Gut Genug!
Liebe, Love, Good Enough!
Liebe! Love!

<u>Day of Deliverance # 3</u>

6/13/23

I got into the program room this morning, it's no later than 8 o'clock as I'm writing this entry right now. It's silent and peaceful, once I'm done writing I will use this area to work on my gifts and talents because I made a promise to prepare to perform when I need to at my best. God has taught me that I can do anything, just have faith and trust in him to guide and have control because a father always provides for his children. Giving whatever is needed in encouragement, confidence, purpose, passion, inspiration, and motivation to overcome any obstacle with perseverance, love, bravery, courage, and heart. Even if the room is empty, I can fill it with Truth, serving God, the Most High Father fully with humility, his Kingdom, and by doing that I will reach a promised Great Future of True Freedom. Despite where I am at, in this jail in Eau Claire. I feel free and peaceful in my Heart. I know with Big G by my side I can change the world, leave a legacy, and achieve my Dreams because I am Good Enough and Destined for Greatness. I pray the Lord gives me a day full of miracles and happiness. Forgiveness!

Ich Bin Gut Genug!

A

m

Good Enough!

D.O.D Diary
P.S - Peaceful Tuesday

Day of Deliverance 3

I figured out what I must do. I know I go to South Minneapolis, MN, and sing serenading to my CHILDHOOD BEST FRIEND, the one who made me confident, and brave, and motivated me to believe in myself. The ONE WHO MADE FEEL WORTHY, GOOD ENOUGH TO LOVE AND BE LOVED. THE ONE WHO INSPIRED ME WITH HER BEAUTY TO HELP OTHERS SO I COULD WIN HEARTS, MY SOULMATE HEAVEN SENT TO MAKE ME A MAN, TO GET TRUE LOVE. I HAVE ALWAYS WANTED TO GET MARRIED AND GIVE MY HEART. THE REASON WHY I BECAME A GENTLEMAN, ATHLETIC, YOUTFUL, GODLY, INTELLECTUAL, FUNNY, GOOD, ARTISTIC, and ENTERTAINING. Also, a LEADER TO UNIFY AND PROVIDE PEACE, LOVE, FREEDOM, AND PROSPERITY FOR MY FAMILY, FRIENDS, SUPPORT, AND THOSE IN NEED. YOU, MADE ME WANT TO BE BETTER!

<u>Final Entry of Day of Deliverance 3</u>

It will be soon time to lock in here at the Detention Center. I will finish reading up to Acts chapter 15 before I lay down to fall asleep. I was just in the "classroom," working on improving my barriers to gain confidence and courage so I can be prepared at a time and situation to perform to the best of my ability even when nervous. Today was an amazing day, I have signed the application

for "Hope Gospel Mission." Also, today was the 25th anniversary for them, they were on television and the crazy thing is I had my Holy Bible when it came on the news. Everything happens for a reason, I do believe that God, or I call the Most High Father "Big G," just know it wasn't a coincidence because I later received the application from the Deputy O. after shortly. I am confident that this is the next step in my life to get back home to the Twin Cities in Minnesota to my family and friends. Well, I'm about to get my reading in. Then get ready to sleep and brush my teeth after having a snack. I pray for another day.

D.O.D Diary
#PAIDTUESDAY

<u>Day of Deliverance 4</u>

6/14/23

It's Wednesday Morning, I'm writing in my diary early waiting for the door to the cell to unlock and open, the lights to turn on. I'm sitting on the floor in the corner to the corner close to where I'm technically in front of my cell I1. I have had decent rest, I fumbled, tossed, and kept waking up out of my sleep. I figured because it was the signs I needed to get up and prepare for my day. I hope mental health comes to see me today, so I can move back to medium today if Big G allows it, and if not, I am content with that as well. I would like to finish something

before court tomorrow Thursday, June 15th. The Deputy just came by to do a routine check-up, they do it about every 30 – 60 minutes. It depends on where you at whether you are classified High, Medium, Low, or Mental Health (Special Needs). Now, don't judge me, I have admitted earlier and mentioned where I am at. I'm not to the point where I'm a danger to myself and others. It's quite funny how I ended up here.

I started praying to my Most High Power, Father God (Big G), I prayed for my loved ones (Family and Friends), and then I started to weep from Happiness, Love, and caring for those who are family and friends. Then the ONE I HAVE NEVER STOP LOVING, pictures and visuals of her BEAUTIFULNESS MADE ME WEEP MORE. I PRAYED FOR HER AND HER FAMILY, I ASKED BIG G TO STAY BY HER SIDE. THAT'S WHEN THINGS BECAME CLEAR, I KNEW SHE WAS MY FATIMA, A WOMAN OF THE DESERT THAT I HAVE TO RETURN TO, MY HOME. I got up from my knees with tears in my eyes and unashamed because they were not of anger, were of MISSING SOMEONE SPECIAL THAT GIVE ME DRIVE AND DETERMINATION TO GET NEXT TO THEM AND BE BETTER, DOING THE RIGHT THING. IT'S NOT BAD To MISS THEM. WHEN YOU CRY OR WEEP, IT'S FROM TRULY CARING, LOVING, AND WANTING GOOD FOR THEM, AND A LIFE OF PEACE, HAPPINESS, AND PROSPERITY. "Happy Tears," I went to the classroom and sang, rapped did octaves I thought didn't know or was able to do. That's why I am here and I WEPT UNASHAMED.

D.O.D Diary
#HappyTearsWEDNESDAY

Day of Deliverance 4E

One of my favorite shows, "Riverdale," came on CW TV at 8 o'clock central time, and before that was "Nancy Drew," another show I watched today from "Anfang, Start" to Ende, Finish." I thought it would be cool to include some German in this entry. After I finished watching my shows, I took about a half hour at the most using the shower before lock-in for the night. I have planned it that way anyway, it went accordingly. I feel nice and comfortable, at peace with everything in this moment as I sit my spot where I sat the night before writing my last entry of the day. I read the Holy Bible or "The Word" or my "Sword of God," today strengthen my mind, body, and soul with the "Good News" or "Scripture." It was amazing, right before I wrote "amazing," I had to pause being the door caught my attention to our "Mod" or "Block," which opened coincidently just as I finished writing the word "was." "There's no such thing as coincidences, things happen for a reason," my close friend used to say all the time. I had to pause for a few minutes because I had to remember how much she helped me, which is why I saying, "I love you!" I pray God is giving you everything needed because you are a strong, intelligent, beautiful, and amazing woman." I hope one day we cross paths again. Good Night!

D.O.D Diary
#6/14/2023

<u>Day of Deliverance 5</u>

6/15/23

Today is the day, it's about 6 o'clock central time here in Wisconsin. I have court later at 9:30 am, at least that is what it says on my paperwork for court from my public defender. I am weirdly shaken because I feel some type of energy. It's not from nervousness, I had to pray to stop shaking and refocus myself as I wrote this journal entry this morning. This shaking sensation had a strange feeling of excitement like my brother from another was shaken the same way when he got bailed out. At least that is what he told me, however according to humans, you're supposed to "Believe half of what you see and nothing you hear." That sight gave me more hope and faith and belief that he would change things around for me too. I am ready to change my life and work hard enough, putting life's plans into action. I have earned a certificate in "Creative Writing," finished my "Re-Entry," packet which I must meet with the teacher for my certificate, and I will finish my packet for "Parenting," earning my certificate. I must go to "Literacy Chippewa Valley," to do that, which I will. I pray for the Lord to bless me. I have faith!

The lights just turned on, the door to the block has closed, and in a bit too, the door will open, this all happens in sync after another. The deputies just announced, "Roll call and breakfast" and then the TV in the block turned on. I have gotten up brushed my teeth, drank some fluids for hydration, read my "Sword of God" or the "Holy Bible," prayed, and read daily bread news this morning while I prepare for the day. I took a shower last night so I could be ready for my day and clean for the Judge in court, however, I am also clear and clean-minded, sober. I feel like I went through a "40-Day Fast," I have faith in my Lord Jesus Christ that "Big G," the Most High Power God, the Father will make a way for me. Today is still a blessing because I still have a chance to change! However, I am prepared without expectations! Until Later Maybe! Breakfast is coming now!

D.O.D Diary
Court/ Judgement Day
June 15, 2023! Great
Thursday Morning Blessed!
Full of Hope, Prepared for the Worst!
#HAPPY 43 DAYS!

<u>Day of Deliverance 6</u>

6/16/23

I prayed for patience. Also, for forgiveness, I had to take a break and pause to center myself, and my feelings/emotions. I don't want to be distracted by those who want to play the wrong games, with bad intentions of people of negative outcomes. I did not write yesterday after my last entry. So, you probably guessed that I am still here incarcerated in Eau Claire Jail, if you did then that's a trait of being able to figure out things. Yesterday was an amazing day, full of blessings, I have gotten good news and understanding that I will be released on my next court date. I also hope I will get to move back to medium. If today is the day our service leader, the woman of God does the Sundays over in the area I'm at right now. She also does music which is something we have in common. I performed a demo in which she said, "That was beautiful." I cannot lie I was a little nervous, but it became easier.

Yesterday went smoothly and I got a one-on-one visit with the chaplain people, it went great. I slept in peace after that night. This morning didn't start so well, but it's been overturned by music, prayer, and God.

It was unusual today, done with my case in Eau Claire, and I'm released from here, however, I must wait to see what St. Croix will do with me. I sent a message on the kiosk to my probation to inform them of the situation so I can prevent a future warrant with Eau Claire. I still have to deal with the present, right now. I just need to live in the moment. One is okay with the current situation and will not ruin my peace.

Final Day of Deliverance 6

I just wrote probation a letter before this entry. It is about 9:30 (21:30) pm Central Time right now. I know it will soon be "Roll Call" or "Lock-in," for the night. They just announced it on the intercom as finished writing the last sentence. The door after I had written "the door," I had to go inside my cell because I was at first writing this on the table in the block. I am now sitting in my spot where I sit at night while I write before I get ready for bed. I still had a pretty decent Friday. I had some laughs and fun despite still being incarcerated. I guess one must still do time for their wrongs, and definitely will endure because "This shall also pass." I'm still blessed because I can still improve on what I need so I can be my best self.

Day of Deliverance 7

6/17/23

It is Saturday afternoon. Today is my children's mother's birthday, it is ironic how we have gotten double trays during lunch. I have gotten up from the seating area in front of my cell door to slide the trays through the door during pick-up. Today anyway is her 36th birthday, even though we are not together, we always promised to be friends.

I was so mad about how things ended, for a long time. I did get over it because of the tragedy of losing a child, due to death. Child Protection Services (CPS) have taken the only child we had left on earth alive. Rarely do relationships and/or couples survive, more than 97% end in parting and going separate ways. If she ever reads this from my published version, I owe her this as a friend and father of her children, "Thank you for being a great mother to our children and dealing with me. Thanks for taking care of me during my seizures and blackouts. Thanks for loving me as a person. I know I was a little young 'shit' at times. I learned a lot from you. Also, I learned to live and watch you beat addiction because of loving and caring for someone and something. I am glad that you had a couple of my seeds.

I remember the letter you wrote me, the last one when you 'so-called-hated-me.' It did piss me off because it was one of the most encouraging letters I have ever gotten. I was mad because I was wondering with confusion. It did not make sense because I felt every word, knew, and kept my silence. You were right about everything you have written in the letter. The problem is because I blamed myself for our daughter 'S.A.B' and 'N.A.B' getting taken away. I did not ever blame you for any of this that happened to us. I watched you become a real 'Mother,' even when you lost your father and mother while pregnant with our second child. I know you from the inside out, I know when something is wrong, just like you knew when I was not myself. I am laughing because I thought no one paid attention to me much but you saw things in me even my mother did not catch. At least that is what I think. I will always be bonded to you because of our children but also because of my love for you and I am forever thankful to you." There is a reason why I must say to you this. I made a choice and must do it.

"You or the mother don't deserve to be parents," I will not ever forget what the "CPS" worker said to me in front of our daughter with the Sheriff on her left side looking at me with judgmental eyes as well. I knew was wrong because our daughter ran to her grandmother, my mom after if I'm not mistaken looking at the Sheriff. They talked about self-control; I have never told my mom what the b***h said to me. All the CPS worker female saw was a black man who was young and a pretty little light-skinned baby with good hair. I could tell that look from anywhere, I know when is being judged by age, or skin color. The worker already had her mind made up because of slander and/or defamation of character by the "News" on TV, libel, which had influenced the Judge to make his decisions/judgment to take custodial rights from us. I just want to say to my children's mother that you were right about everything. Even though I am incarcerated currently while writing this, just know that I have decided to change my lifestyle.

You asked what is it that I want. I want you to stop blaming yourself because you were a great mother to our children and

I know that you have the strength to overcome what has happened. We were great parents, our second daughter loved us, she wasn't in pain, and she is in Heaven with the Creator with her ancestors who love her. If I was thinking clearly, I would have done this already. I can't change the past but I can control what I do in the present so there is a better altered future. One that helps bring justice and understanding from those who didn't know you. People who don't get a person who is grieving the way they know how to. By the way, we are a couple of parents because of our children, the fact we still get along proves that we overcame the obstacle of losing a child to death, which makes us survivors. I am in Eau Claire County Jail, but I hope you are enjoying your day. I am praying for you, and I love you, HAPPY BIRTHDAY!

Day of Deliverance 7E

I must say, it was a great day. It flowed by smoothly. It is already Sunday in about a wake-up. I went to the classroom to work on music and some writing. I am feeling ready to lock in my cell. I hope that today was blessed for anyone who is reading this. Also, "I hope you had a great Birthday," the mother of my children. "I love you Baby Mama!" in my goofy tone of voice. Yeah, but in all seriousness, I hope that you're safe. I am praying for you and believe in you. Believe in Faith.

D.O.D Diary

P.S - HAPPY BIRTHDAY

M.A.H, June 17th!

Day of Deliverance 8

6/15/23

It's Sunday morning, breakfast coming around, still a little sluggish, however, I am still feeling optimistic about today. I have no worries really besides my case in St. Croix County however it only crossed my mind just as I was writing this entry. That's not important right now, One must get through this day still. No one knows when their time is, only God the Father has it written on his hand. I pray for peace, patience, and a happy day for anyone who would like to have it. I pray for my friends, family, and those in need. Lastly for those who need a sign from God, I pray you get the sign sent to you. Amen!

D.O.D Diary
#Sunday Morning

Day of Deliverance 8A

I have talked to my younger brother. He told me, "Happy Father's Day!" He also paid for my phone call today from jail, he is the one I trust the most. I even told him I had sent him a letter; he hadn't received it yet. I told him that I might have to go to St. Croix County too, maybe if there is not a solution found or dissolved here. It's about 4:15 pm (16:15 in 14hr Time) right now, I looked at the video chat kiosk behind me where I was sitting to get the time. It will be dinner soon here in the jail where I'm at. I might be picked up tomorrow if that's what happens, so I can at least feel better about leaving something unfinished. I have a superstition with that in which I do not want to come back here to finish it. I would rather get it done and move on to what I need to do next and keep moving forward with life.

Day of Deliverance 8E

It is 8:47 pm (20:47 in 24hr Time), and we are still waiting to go to church service. I am stationed in the spot I sit at, inside my cell at night when I am writing before I get ready for bed.

I had to pause to watch the rest of "UP," the movie so I could focus on this entry to close this day. It is now about 10 pm, The News just came on, and this month has been filled with Mass Shootings, war, natural disasters, etc. I still keep up on what's going on outside doing time for the crimes I committed. Today went by as smoothly as the whole weekend did. The church service was amazing, and the leader was great I great singing I sang too. It felt great I feel like just did an audition for "American Idol," "America Got Talent" or even "The Voice." I feel uplifted. I will get to celebrate with my children this holiday, Father's Day. I know it with all my children including my first-born, my little Diva. I know we will meet again baby girl just know you might have more siblings and they will love you like I do. Until then, I promise I am going to do whatever it takes to get you back because I have a plan. I like to follow the plans God has put on my heart. God the Most High Father I trust in Him because he has never wronged me. I pray that believe, love, and trust in God too. He will bring us back together because there's no bond like Father and Daughter!

D.O.D Diary
#FATHER'S DAY
P.S. - Keep Moving
Forward (KMF)

<u>Day of Deliverance 9</u>

6/19/23

Today is Juneteenth but, to me, it is a birthday to someone I hold dear to me. Someone who has seen me do things no one has. One of the people who can bring me out of the darkness because she has a good heart. She is one of the strongest women that I love and care about. We understand each other because it takes someone who is not normal to be able to get to know us, we are rare. The Capricorn and the Gemini have a legendary chemistry that is powerful and historical. I always followed her around when as a younger man. We sometimes did not have to say much to know things about how we were feeling or how life was treating us! They say 98% of communication is non-verbal and if you have a connection like that hold that person dear to you. Whether they end up a lover or a friend or in your family, a relationship like that is unique and so uncommon. She may be "Rude," but that's a bond I keep inside. I pray that she gets to have a very wonderful day that is amazing, peaceful, loving, and happy because she deserves it. This is a day in my heart I cannot forget. I will not ever forget her. You know hearts, you know her heart. You know it is good. Amen! Let this day be full of wonders, I love you!

D.O.D Diary
P.S. - HAPPY BIRTHDAY S.M.H!

Day of Deliverance 9A

Last week was weird as I reflect, a lot of things have gotten backed up. I just prayed over the meals that we were about to receive. I am thankful we at least get to eat because other prisons/jails are worst around the world. I am however getting annoyed with mental health playing me like a fool and keeping their word with me. It is irritating that they think it will cause me to act out of character. No, I will not make it worse, but I can use my words to express myself because I know how to translate my feelings and emotions on paper. I do not need to use vulgar language to explain either. This is ridiculous, when I was in addiction, someone could use that they were coming off the chemicals. What excuse do you have now? I am sober and clear-headed, with self-control and the ability to make smart decisions. I do not have anything altering my thinking, so what is your excuse of being a liar then? There are not any, I feel that an opinion based on a potential worry is not a fact. Let's speak facts please and comprehend each other points. Let us figure this out and resolve this situation. Just know this won't ruin my day at all. I am stronger than this!

D.O.D Diary
#Afternoon Troubles
of being Annoyed

Day of Deliverance 9B

I just got done watching M.A.S.H., until the commercial break. I was staring at the page after I wrote the title on top. The entry I wrote earlier today around noon, was just to show how no one has a perfect day. Today still went by pretty smoothly and was good. "The Rising," just came back on from the commercial break, I do not watch television much, at least not all day. Also, I just thought I would write this down in "black and white."

D.O.D Diary

#Good Day

<u>Day of Deliverance 10</u>

6/20/23

This morning I must admit I'm still a little tired. I am wondering how today will play out. Would I get moved to medium or will St. Croix County come and get me today? I do not know the answer to these questions but, I do know one thing. I am closer to my freedom. I know I will appreciate it this time, do the things I need to turn it around for the better because I do not want to come here behind these walls dressed in orange. I don't want the withdrawals of fentanyl and heroin. The high is not worth nor is the troubles. That is why I am waiting patiently right now because I must but also because I know the next step. Happy Tuesday Morning! Everyday! It is a blessing!

D.O.D Diary
#Happy Tuesday

Day of Deliverance 10A

I took a nap after breakfast, read Esther 1-2, wrote in my journal/diary, and watched the news this morning. One of my cellmates had a meeting concerning court and has not come yet. I am full of hope that God has made a way for him. It is good news however that he is one step closer than he was yesterday, even though it was not court in front of a judge.

Chicago Fire is on right now and we are all back. Even "A.G," is now back in the cell block, we are all waiting for lunch to come right now. This is what it is like in life when you deal with the present, it becomes what is important. Right now, is what's important, at this moment. I finally got another helpful answer, so I know what to expect and also what not to expect.

#GoodTuesdayAnswers

Day of Deliverance 10B

I was watching "Chicago Fire," the TV show on "ION." I am waiting for the supplies for cleaning, it is different here in "Mental Health/Special Needs." We get the cleaning supplies every other day. I am the only one up in the cell block.

The beautiful Deputy Correctional Officer "Ms. O," brought the cleaning supplies. Giving us about an hour to have it all done including our cells, common area, and shower. I announced it to my cellmates. We all worked together as a team to get it all done in about half that time. I would say in like 33 minutes at the most.

<u>Day of Deliverance 10E</u>

So, it is after 10 o'clock right now. I have been transported to St. Croix County Jail in the city of Hudson, Wisconsin. I have been brought from 500 (Mental Health) to the booking area, where the transport cell is also at. Accompanied by two beautiful Deputies Ms. O and the new officer in training with the amazing smile and glasses that make her just as beautiful without them.

I can say this, The Eau Claire County Deputies I dealt with have been amazing. I really mean it. This is the smoothest time I have ever had. Believe I did more time than this before, but I have never had an experience like Eau Claire Jail. It is a correctional facility.

D.O.D Diary
#GBye ECC!

"My Prospective Journey"

Days of Deliverance

12/12/23

It's now December 12, 2023, and as I back over the last six months of my life, I see myself being incarcerated in Eau Claire then St. Croix County Jail, writing, learning, and journaling. Longing to come to Minnesota. Longing to change my life. Gaining my purpose and realizing my life's goal which is to provide, guide, and serve. Help give others a chance that could change their lives. I want to be the proof that God the Creator exists, taking the throne being the Golden Child and a Man of God spreading love throughout the world. I was released to the outside on August 2nd. I am currently dealing with probation and outpatient with the hopes of early dismissal. I have also made mistakes being out of here and still need help in some areas. I have learned and worked and am still in the process of learning and working the tools and wisdom to my freedom back. My relationships are rekindling. I am also making more connections to be successful. I no longer look at life as if it is going against me. No longer am I afraid of taking chances and being confident in myself. I'm still learning to surrender, "let go and let God." Trusting in God, myself, and the right people.

I am content and at peace, looking down on my last six months, I'm learning to love myself again. I see progress, growth, actions. Before I was fighting the way I knew, just to do so, rejecting anything new or unknown. Now I see that I'm fighting for love, peace, happiness, and prosperity. For the greater good.

I will give grace and give my heart to the people who deserve it. With all the hopes of leaving behind a legacy.

D.O.D Diary

<u>Last of Days of Deliverance</u>

12/26/23

So, the month is almost done. I have successfully typed my diary I have made it in Eau Claire County along with the poems. I did lose motivation while writing this and had to find it back again and again. I feel indescribable right now, I can't believe I have done it. It is almost 3 o'clock afternoon right now and I have outpatient at 5 pm. I'm sitting in my mother's room with her kitten to the right of me. I am ready to walk into the next year and proud of how far have come. The Most High has blessed me. I will start next year with keys to my own apartment, stability, and even more next year. I know where I am going but, I do not honestly know what's my next chapter. I'm just taking a day at a time. My first official is done!

D.O.D Diary

The End!

About the Author

I was born in the south side of Chicago as Pierre Denzel Bowdry. I grew up in South Minneapolis, graduated from South Senior High, and studied abroad in Herford, Germany winning a CBYX for YFU(2012-2013), having an amazing host family and to learn about German language and culture. Life has been an unexpected journey since coming back to the states, having two beautiful daughters on 9/22/16 and 12/02/17. Experiencing the tragedies loss of children through adoption and death. I begin living in homelessness, addiction, and crime. In and out of incarceration until landing in a cell away from home in another state. Sobering up forced thoughts of my past and trauma. Eventually rediscovered goals. Writing helped find purpose and as an inmate was able to earn a certificate in Creative Writing.